D0177857

HEM

Please renew or return items by the date
shown on your receipt

www.hertfordshire.gov.uk/libraries

Renewals and enquiries: 0300 123 4049

Textphone for hearing or 0300 123 4041
speech impaired users:

L32 11.16

529 878 32 6

Anne Cathrine Bomann lives in Copenhagen, where she divides her time between writing and working as a psychologist. She also played table tennis for Denmark and won the national championship twelve times. *Agatha* is her debut novel, following two poetry collections. First published in Denmark, it became a word-of-mouth success and has now been translated into twenty-three languages.

Agatha

Anne Cathrine Bomann

Translated from the Danish by Caroline Waight

SCEPTRE

Originally published in Danish in 2017 by Braendpunkt, Denmark, as *Agathe*
First published in Great Britain in 2019 by Sceptre
An Imprint of Hodder & Stoughton
An Hachette UK company

1

A CIP catalogue record for this title is available from the British Library

Hardback ISBN 9781529361377
eBook ISBN 9781529361391

Typeset in Sabon MT Std 11.5/17.75 pt by
Palimpsest Book Production Limited, Falkirk, Stirlingshire

Printed and bound in Great Britain by Clays Ltd, Elcograf S.p.A.

Hodder & Stoughton policy is to use papers that are natural,
renewable and recyclable products and made from wood grown in
sustainable forests. The logging and manufacturing processes are expected
to conform to the environmental regulations of the country of origin.

Hodder & Stoughton Ltd
Carmelite House
50 Victoria Embankment
London EC4Y 0DZ

www.sceptrebooks.co.uk

Maths

Retiring at seventy-two meant that there were five months still to work. Twenty-two weeks in total, and if all my patients came that meant I had exactly eight hundred sessions to go. If somebody cancelled or fell ill, the number would of course be fewer. There was a certain comfort in that, in spite of everything.

Panes

I was sitting in the front room peering out of the window when something happened. The spring sun lay across my carpet in four staggered squares, moving slowly but surely over my feet. At my side was an unopened first edition of Sartre's *Nausea,* which I'd been trying to get into for years. Her legs were thin and pale, and I was surprised she was allowed out in only a dress this early in the year. She had drawn a hopscotch grid on the road and was hopping deep in concentration, first on one leg then on both, before switching back again. Her hair was gathered into two pigtails, she was probably seven or thereabouts, and she lived with her mother and an older sister further up the road at number four.

You may be thinking I was some kind of philosophical savant, sitting at the window all day long, contemplating things far greater than hopscotch and the wanderings of the sun across the floor. You would be wrong. In fact I was sitting there because I had nothing better to do, and perhaps also because there was something life-affirming about the triumphant exclamations that now and then drifted through to me when the girl had executed a particularly difficult combination of hops.

At some point I went to make a cup of tea, and when I returned to my post she was gone. She'd probably come up with a more entertaining game elsewhere, I thought; chalk and stone had both been left in the middle of the street.

And that was when it happened. I'd just set down the cup to cool on the windowsill and spread the rug over my knees when I noticed something falling on the edge of my field of vision. At the moment a shrill scream reached my ears, I'd coaxed my stiff body back onto its feet and stepped up close to the window. She was lying at the foot of a tree, a little way down the road to my right, where the path turns off towards the lake. On one of the branches I caught sight of a cat swinging its tail. Below, the girl had raised herself into a sitting position, her back against the trunk, while she held her ankle and sobbed.

I pulled my head back. Should I go to her? I hadn't spoken to a child since I was one myself, and that hardly counted. Would it not just make her more upset if a strange man suddenly appeared and tried to comfort her? I stole another glance outside; she was still sitting in the grass, her tear-stained face peering down the road, past my house.

It was probably best nobody saw me. Isn't that the doctor? they would say to one another. Why is he just gawping like that? So I took my teacup and went into the kitchen, settled at the table. Although I told myself the girl would soon get up and hobble home, that everything was fine, I still sat there like a fugitive in my own kitchen as the hours passed.

The tea went cold and cloudy, and darkness fell before at last I crept back into the front room and, half-hidden behind the curtain, squinted down the road. By then, of course, she was gone.

Traces

Madame Surrugue had greeted me in the same way every single morning since I took her on. Day after day she sat at the big mahogany desk like a queen upon her throne, and as I walked through the door she would rise to take my stick and coat, while I placed my hat on the shelf above the coat rack. Then she would run through the day's schedule and finally hand me a sheaf of case files, which were otherwise punctiliously archived in a large system of shelves behind the desk. We exchanged a few more words, then as a rule I didn't see her again before 12.45 p.m., when I left the office and went to take my lunch at a mediocre restaurant nearby.

When I returned she was always sitting precisely as I'd left her, and occasionally I'd wonder whether she ate at all. There was no sniff of food, and I'd never seen so much as a crumb underneath her desk. Did Madame Surrugue even require sustenance to live?

That morning she told me a German woman had phoned and wanted to come by later to make an appointment.

'I've spoken to Dr Durand about her. Apparently she was admitted to Saint Stéphane with severe mania after a suicide attempt a few years ago.'

'No,' I said firmly. 'We can't accept her. She would take years to treat.'

'Dr Durand also believes she ought to be re-admitted, but apparently she insists on consulting with you, Doctor. I could easily find space for her in the schedule?'

Madame Surrugue looked enquiringly at me, but I shook my head.

'No, it can't be done. Kindly direct her to seek help elsewhere.'

By the time I retired I would have been practising

for nearly fifty years, and that was more than enough. The last thing I needed was a new patient.

Madame Surrugue eyed me a moment longer, but then continued going through the day without pursuing the subject.

'Thank you, that's fine,' I said, taking the sheaf of case files and heading into my office. It was situated at the very opposite end of Madame Surrugue's dominion, the large reception area where the patients could wait their turn, so neither my secretary's clacking typewriter nor any conversation between herself and the patients disturbed me while I worked.

My first patient, a woman by the name of Madame Gainsbourg, dry as dust, had just arrived and was flicking through one of the magazines Madame Surrugue occasionally brought. Sighing a little too deeply, I reminded myself that after hers there were only seven hundred and fifty-three conversations to go.

The day passed anchorless until I returned to the office after lunch and nearly bumped into a deathly pale, dark-haired woman standing just inside the doorway. I apologised for my clumsiness. The woman was strikingly slender, her eyes enormous in her pointed face.

'It's quite all right, I'm the one in the way,' she said, walking further into the room. 'I've come to ask for an appointment.'

She spoke with an unmistakeable accent, and I realised this must be the German woman. She was clutching a map with Saint Stéphane's insignia to her chest.

'I'm afraid that won't be possible,' I replied, but the woman took a rapid step towards me and said earnestly: 'It's absolutely vital I get an appointment. I'm sorry to be a nuisance, but I have nowhere else to go. Please, if you could help me . . .'

Instinctively I stepped backwards. Her brown eyes shone fever-bright and her gaze was so intense it felt as though she'd grabbed my arms. Clearly it would take a battle to be rid of her, and I had neither the time nor the energy. Gesturing towards Madame Surrugue, I tried to force a friendly smile.

'If Madame would be kind enough to follow me,' I said, edging my way around the woman, 'my secretary will be able to explain the circumstances in more detail.'

It was Madame Surrugue's fault the woman was here in the first place, so it was only proper she should turn her away again.

I slipped past the woman, who thankfully followed me over to the desk, where I parked her in front of Madame Surrugue with an eloquent glance.

My secretary raised her left eyebrow a few milli-metres.

'Would you be so kind as to take over, Madame Surrugue?' I enquired, before nodding stiffly in parting and hastening into the safety of my office.

But the image of the pale woman wouldn't leave me be, and the rest of the day it was as though a trace of her perfume lingered in the air, whirling like dust each time I opened my door.

Uproar

Time ran through me like water through a rusty filter nobody troubled to change. I had spoken to seven patients that day with minimal concentration, and had only one left still to go on that leaden, rainy afternoon before I could go home.

Before I accompanied Madame Almeida into my office, I shot my secretary a glance. She was sitting very quietly at the uncluttered desk, staring down at its surface. The Anglepoise lamp cast her stony shadow onto the wall behind her, and she looked so dejected that for a moment I considered whether I ought to say something. But what? Instead I drew the door shut behind me and turned towards my patient.

Madame Almeida, who was nearly a head taller than I and thus always made something of an impression, disburdened herself of her umbrella and rain cape with frantic movements and plumped down on the couch. She smoothed her vomit-toned skirts and eyed me reproachfully through the small glasses balanced on the tip of her crooked nose.

'I have had a dreadful week, Doctor,' she proclaimed, settling herself on the couch. 'I agitate myself so. It's my nerves, I can assure you of that, and I said the same to Bernard – Bernard, I said, you make me nervous simply sitting there in your chair all day long!'

Madame Almeida was always nervous. For her there were no good days. She didn't seem to be getting anything whatsoever out of therapy, yet she still came marching in faithfully twice a week to scold me. The mere notion of a better existence seemed to upset her, and frankly I found it hard to understand why she came at all. Normally I just let her talk, but occasionally I would interject a remark or hazard an interpretation, which she entirely ignored.

'. . . and then she said I owed her three francs

from last week – three francs, if you please, the cheek of it! It really got to me. I nearly had a turn right there in the middle of the shop, but then I told her, I said . . .'

Many years' training helped me to murmur in the right places without actually listening, and if I was lucky I wouldn't have registered a single word by the time she left the room.

Looking down I realised I'd bored the tip of the pencil through the paper in sheer frustration, so I started one of my bird caricatures instead.

'I may have sensitive nerves, but I won't put up with impudence, I can tell you that much!' Madame Almeida was almost yelling. Outside, the rain was so violent it was impossible to see anything but blurry contours through the windows, and unfortunately the droplets beating against the panes seemed to be encouraging my patient to speak even more loudly than usual. But evidently I have to put up with trivialities, I thought resignedly, as I focused on a spot on the crown of her head that looked suspiciously thin of hair. It delighted me to think she might be balding, in which case I would have known long before she did, and I promptly added the detail to my drawing. I imagined her catching a glimpse of herself from behind one day, frozen between a mirror and a windowpane, her podgy fingers frantically scrabbling, pushing the hair aside and exposing the scalp, as she screamed, 'Bernard! Why didn't you say anything, Bernard?' And so, this way or that, there passed another hour of my life. Madame Almeida thanked me for the consultation, and as I held the door for her I carefully angled the notepad away so that she wouldn't catch sight of the balding ostrich.

Six hundred and eighty-eight conversations left. Just then it felt like six hundred and eighty-eight too many.

Growing pains

One morning a few days later I had to cut Madame Surrugue short as she was going through my schedule: 'Wait, what was that? Did the German woman get an appointment after all?'

She inclined her head in a single resolute nod.

'Yes, she was very persistent, I must say. She's adamant about starting therapy, and she's clearly heard good things about you, Doctor.'

I snorted – when had that been reason enough to countermand my instructions?

'I did explain that you would only be here for

another six months. She accepted that unreservedly, so I thought it would be silly to say no.'

She was right. If the German woman was content with just six months, then there was nothing unethical about taking her on, and I ought to be glad of the extra money. Yet I couldn't shake off my irritation. How dare Madame Surrugue squeeze yet another person into my life – against my express wishes – just as I was trying to clear the decks?

But the woman, whose name was apparently Agatha Zimmermann, had been given an appointment at 3 p.m. on the following day, and there didn't seem much more I could do about it.

Once the final patient of the day had left the office, I went out to find Madame Surrugue, who was packing up her things. She looked at me as though searching for something, and asked if it had been a hard day. I shrugged, remarking that it had been like so many others before it. I was still angry with her, but I waited until she'd gathered up her belongings and put on her jacket so I could hold the door for her.

'Thank you,' she said, walking out into the barely perceptible mizzle.

I nodded and locked the door behind us.

'Thank *you*. Good evening.'

'Good evening, Monsieur. See you tomorrow.'

On the way home my legs were tugging me in two different directions. One, I imagined, just wanted to carry me home, where I could eat some bread, settle in my comfortable chair and put my feet up on the footstool while I listened to Bach and let the night come. The other was restless, reminding me of the growing pains I had as a child. My knees had ached so badly I cried, but my father scarcely glanced up from the picture he was working on as he said, 'You're just growing up. It'll pass.'

Perhaps it felt the call of foreign lands, my leg. It had never been further afield than Paris, much less crossed any national borders. Now I was so old it would never happen, and the ache was permanent.

In any case, it was I who set my course, and I directed my halting steps through the evening chill until I reached the garden gate at No. 9 Rue des Rosettes. The street smelled insistently of newly turned soil; several of my neighbours had laid flower-beds and spent hours weeding and planting seeds. Meanwhile I tended stubborn islands of moss, which grew like ripples in the sea of lawn.

Once I'd eaten and the soft bowing of the violins expanded into the space around me like cotton wadding, I was ambushed by a train of thought that had grown increasingly intrusive. And although I recognised that, although I knew how miserable it would make me, I let it come. Somehow it was what I wanted, to sit all alone and feel sorry for myself. Why – it always started the same way – does nobody tell you what happens to the body as it grows old? About the sore joints, the surplus skin, the invisibility? Aging, I thought, as the bitterness flushed through me, was mainly about observing the differences between one's self and one's body get bigger and bigger until eventually one awakes a total stranger to oneself. What was beautiful or natural about that?

And just as the record came to an end and the silence left me alone in the front room, came the fatal blow: there was no way out. I had to live in this traitorous grey prison until it killed me.

Saint Stéphane
Montpellier, 21 June 1935

Re: Agatha Zimmermann

Patient largely non-communicative since
admittance this morning, much of below
drawn from her old medical records.

Case history:
25-year-old German woman, immigrated to
France in 1929 for her studies. Self-
harming behaviour and suicide attempt as
15-year-old and seen regularly by local
doctor Dr Weinrich throughout adoles-
cence.

Patient from a wealthy family with
mother, father and sister two years
younger. No family history of psychologic-
al illness except for an aunt on the
father's side, who spent most of her
adult life at a madhouse in Vienna.
Father blind but self-employed, mother
housewife.

Currently:

Patient admitted today after having applied to own doctor complaining of deep melancholy and thoughts of suicide. Nonetheless opposes admittance. Presenting as hysterical and dramatic. Restraints used. Patient is pale, undernourished and has scratches on her face. Also missing tufts of hair.

Patient is virtually non-communicative, but shouts and cries when she's left alone.

Allergies: None known.

Forward plan: Psychosis (dem. praecox) must be considered, patient observed over next several days. Ether to be given as needed and chloral hydrate, 20 mg at night.

Consult. Phys. M. Durand

Agatha I

'So, we meet again. Do come in, Madame Zimmermann.' I squeezed her much-too-cold hand. She wore a brown skirt and a shapeless black blouse with a roll-neck that looked to be at least a few sizes too big for her spindly body. The intense gaze from the day before was gone, and at the moment it was difficult to see how she could have defeated both Dr Durand and Madame Surrugue. Perhaps I could get shot of her after all.

'Do take a seat on the couch, Madame, and make yourself comfortable.' I gestured towards the green couch and settled myself in the deep leather armchair, whose brown seat was worn so shiny that in places it was almost black.

'Thank you, but first of all you must promise to stop calling me Madame Zimmermann. I'd be grateful if you could call me Agatha.'

It wasn't my custom to call married patients by their Christian names, but it couldn't hurt to humour her. 'As you wish.'

She smiled briefly and threw a glance around the room, which apart from the armchair and couch contained a desk and chair as well as two tall book-cases full of books I'd once collected and read with great zeal. Then she sat down gingerly, turned, and finally lay down on her back.

'Good. I'd actually like to start by reiterating my suggestion that you seek help elsewhere,' I began. 'As you know, I'm retiring in less than six months, and to be frank I'm unlikely to be able to cure you in so short a time. You would be better served by finding someone who can see you throughout your treatment, a doctor in Paris, perhaps.'

Agatha shot bolt upright and exclaimed, 'Out of the question! I won't go into hospital or take any medicine; I need somebody to talk to, and I've decided it should be you.' Her chin jutting, she stared directly into my eyes with a look that said I'd have to drag her out by the hair if I wanted to be rid of her. I sighed and nodded.

'If that's truly what you want.'

'It is!'

'Excellent. If it proves necessary, I shall recommend one of my colleagues once our time together is over.' She shrugged as though it were quite inconsequential, and lay back down again. She wiped her nose with a rapid gesture. Then she lay still.

'In that case,' I continued, 'I suggest we see each other twice weekly, Tuesday at 3 p.m. and Friday at 4 p.m., one hour each session. My fee is 30 francs per hour. If you are prevented from coming you are welcome to cancel, but I will invoice you for every hour of treatment until the day you choose not to return.'

She nodded. Again I noticed the scent of her perfume, a waft of spices that occasionally skimmed past my nose. What *did* it remind me of?

'Good. You should feel confident telling me everything you feel. Concealment and lies only delay the process, and nothing we talk about will ever leave this room.'

As always, I concluded my little monologue with

a sentence meant to invite the patient into the conversation: 'And now I'd like to hear more about what's bothering you.'

Agatha hesitated, screwing up her eyes slightly.

'I have come,' she said in her marked accent – perhaps that was why she spoke so painstakingly that all the syllables were clear as crystal – 'because I've lost the desire to live again. I cherish no illusions about getting better, but I'd like to be able to function.'

Evidently I was dealing with that rarest of things – someone who wasn't asking for miracles. The vast majority of my patients wanted happy, problem-free lives, but that wasn't my stock-in-trade.

'And what's preventing you from functioning?' I asked.

Agatha began telling me about her symptoms. She had headaches and eczema, she cried often, and was subject to abrupt and violent fits of rage. She slept either too much or not at all, and she could no longer cope with her work as a bookkeeper for an accountant in the city. After calling in sick a few weeks ago she'd spent most of her days crying, shouting at her husband Julian or lying in bed in the foetal position. I listened distractedly to her complaints while I tried to think of what it was she smelled of.

'Sometimes,' she said dreamily, 'I fantasise about scratching myself bloody or disfiguring myself so that nobody would recognise me.'

The juxtaposition between the violent words and her total lack of facial expression was striking.

'Indeed?'

'I get this urge to blot out my face; I don't deserve it.'

'Do you wish you had a different one?' I asked, but she shook her head.

'No. I just have to be struck out.'

I made a brief note on my pad and sighed again. It was as I'd foreseen: she was seriously ill, and it would be impossible to help her in the few months I had left. I cursed my wilful secretary; because of her I'd been lumped with a stubborn, mentally disturbed woman who had clearly got it into her head that I could save her from herself.

'I understand,' I said, 'and I'll do my very best to help you, Madame. Let's stop here for today, and we'll see each other again on Friday at 4 p.m.'

'Thank you, Doctor,' said Agatha earnestly as we shook hands in parting. 'That means a lot.'

Saint Stéphane
Montpellier, 20 August 1935

Re: Agatha Zimmermann

Patient prevented today 8.12 a.m. from committing suicide with razor blade.

Unknown how she acquired it. Managed to cut rt. wrist before found by Nurse Mme Linée. Given 8 stitches with silk thread to be removed in 10—14 days.

Currently restrained and to remain so until calm again.

Treatment attempted first with ether and later with ECT since admittance on 21 June. Has been less tearful, but largely presents as apathetic and vague when communicating, apart from individual hysterical attacks. Shows no obvious psychotic symptoms, observations instead indicate manic depression.

Forward plan:

Continue ECT treatment and ether at night and during attacks. No trips out or visits, and restraints to be maintained except during supervised meals. If patient continues her anorexic regime, force-feeding is permitted.

Consult. Phys. M. Durand

The invisible friend

My neighbour played the piano. Not often, but always the same clumsy piece, as though he couldn't really play but had learned that one melody off by heart. I didn't know what it was called, but in time I grew fond of it, and occasionally I caught myself humming along while I was tidying up after a meal or boiling water for my tea.

After an especially long and futile day at the office I fell asleep early in my chair, lulled by the slow tinkling on the other side of the wall, the kind of wall that fosters closeness even as it separates. For we knew each other, he and I. We'd lived side by side for so many years that all the little noises were routines we could follow without a second thought – it was time now for the obligatory last visit to the toilet at night, time now to wake and get ready for church. First he was in high spirits, then sad and empty; I imagined I could hear all that from the way he moved his fingers across the keys and in the lacunae between each sign of life. One time a whole weekend went by when I heard not a peep from him, and I grew more and more uneasy. What frightened me most, of course, was that I would soon have to go over and knock, so it was a huge relief when finally I heard a door shut and realised he was still alive.

I doubted I would recognise him if I met him on the street. Mostly I walked lost in my own thoughts, and even if I'd tried to pay attention I wouldn't have known what I was looking for. Was he tall or short? Had he retained his hair? I hadn't a clue. But his rhythms, his ramblings through life, those I knew and recognised. I felt a close connection to him, and although I couldn't really know I was sure he felt the same. Whenever I dropped a mug on the tiled kitchen floor or on the rare occasion when I broke into song, I thought of him. Perhaps he was standing on the other side of the wall, his head cocked, listening. Perhaps one day he'd knock and tell me who I was.

Well, that's the way I thought. I've no doubt this sounds odd – I do understand I come across as a solitary man – but I'd never once considered he might be anything but an invisible friend. Why should we have anything in common in the real world? We played the roles we'd been assigned, two people who happened to be in the same place in a city of twenty thousand, most of whom were strangers to each other.

I'd never been the type to interrupt a pattern already begun, and although there were only twelve metres between his garden gate and mine, it was a detour I would never come to take.

Agatha II

'It's like I'm walking around with one of those trunks, you know, the little kind where girls keep their playthings?'

I hummed affirmatively.

'It's shut, and I clutch it tight to make sure it doesn't open. People around me seeing it imagine it's full of all sorts of stuff – knowledge, good qualities, skills and the like – and as long as it's shut nobody knows the truth. Then suddenly I trip and drop the trunk. It springs open, and that's the moment it's embarrassingly obvious to everybody! The trunk is empty; there's absolutely nothing in it!'

Agatha was lying on her back with her hands folded on her chest, and her eyes were wide as she talked. From the angle I was sitting behind her I could study the tiniest movement, while I myself was comfortably hidden. Her black eyelashes trembled a fraction, her chest swelled rhythmically up and down, but otherwise she was motionless. Her voice flowed, sonorous and easy.

'Mnh,' I murmured again. This unremarkable noise, which made no demands, was usually more than enough to make my patients talk.

'It's terrible!' Her voice grew more forceful. 'I feel like a traitor who's about to be revealed at any moment – it's just a question of who and when. So I stay at home in bed, and suddenly a week has gone by.'

I considered my options. Let her keep talking, ask a question, or offer an intervention. In lieu of something sensible to say, I asked, 'Does anybody know the contents of your trunk? Your husband, for example?'

'Julian and I have a complicated relationship.'

'I see.' Experimenting, I tried another tack. 'What would happen if you opened the trunk yourself, or just left it at home and went out as you are?'

She laughed, but it was a compressed, flat sound that bore no relation to joy.

'Then I might as well disappear, Doctor. The trunk is all I have!'

All this trunk talk was exhausting. My knees hurt and the pressure was building behind my temples. Carefully, so as not to disturb Agatha, I stretched and bent my legs a few times. It helped. Seventeen minutes until I could shut the door behind her and appreciate the day's count, which was heading zero-wards with reassuring determination.

'Tell me a little more about what people think you're hiding in the trunk, Agatha,' I asked absently, adding the outlines of a broken wing to the scruffy sparrow in my notepad.

Water-lilies

One of the very worst things about my job was talking to people who had lost somebody. Give me a bad anxiety attack or the consequences of a difficult upbringing any time; deaths were impossible to deal with, and I never knew what to do with grieving patients.

But when you've been practising for fifty years they're impossible to avoid, and one day Monsieur Ansell-Henry arrived late for a session for the first time during his treatment. Ansell-Henry suffered from compulsive neuroses, and as a rule he was impossible to fault: he came and went on time, he answered the questions that were put to him, and his suit fitted tailored and spotless as though a logical extension of his stiff body. But not today.

'Apologies, Doctor,' he mumbled as he dragged himself into the office nearly twenty minutes late and toppled onto the couch.

'Do come in, Monsieur. I'd nearly given up on seeing you today,' I said, wondering whether Ansell-Henry was unwell. He looked as though he'd just woken up and had come in the clothes he'd slept in, and it was clear he'd neither combed his hair nor shaved.

At that moment he began to sob.

'What on earth has happened?' I asked, but he just shook his head and buried his face in his hands. His whole body was twitching uncontrollably. I looked first at him and then at the closed door, seized by a powerful urge to call for Madame Surrugue. She'd know what ought to be done; this was clearly a matter that required feminine solicitude rather than clinical analysis.

Casting about for something to do, I stood up and fetched a napkin from the wooden box on the shelf.

Then I cleared my throat and said, 'I can see you're

in distress, Monsieur, but if I'm going to help you then you need to tell me what's happened.'

At first I didn't think he would answer, but then he lifted his head slightly.

'Marine is dead,' came the jerky reply between each gasping in-breath. 'She died yesterday.'

Marine was Ansell-Henry's wife, and the only person in the world of whom he was fond. Towards everyone else he was over-punctilious and reserved, but somehow she had managed to penetrate his armour. My patient sat up, took the napkin and dried his eyes before vehemently blowing his nose. Then he blinked, a little confused, and looked at me properly for the first time. I returned his gaze, but didn't know what to say. What did he want from me? My hands were like restive animals in my lap, and I grabbed the left one firmly with the right and squeezed.

'I'm sorry to hear that,' I said.

He nodded, but didn't break eye contact. Could he tell I was struggling? Was it obvious I had no idea how to help him?

'Everybody knows that during periods of deep grieving such as this, one may regress to earlier phases,' I began, sensing myself speak faster and faster. 'You may find you become angrier than usual, or that you lose interest in day-to-day matters for a while. This is completely natural, and you mustn't be afraid. It will pass.' I sent him what I hoped was an encouraging smile. 'All of it will pass in time.'

Ansell-Henry frowned. Unable to hold his gaze any longer, I glanced at my notepad instead, jotting down a few random words.

'My wife is due to be buried in three days. The only person I have ever loved is dead.' His voice, thick with tears, cracked. 'And you're telling me it will pass?'

Instantly my mouth was so dry it was like moving my tongue through glue.

'I didn't mean it like that,' I forced myself to say. 'I'm terribly sorry for your loss, Monsieur.' That was all I had. I gestured with my arms. 'May I suggest we postpone our conversations until you're feeling up to it again?'

The balled-up napkin he'd flung onto the table as he walked out was slowly un-crumpling. I followed its movements with my eyes as the minutes passed, and for some reason I couldn't shake myself out of the moment. Even when it was completely still, like a solitary water-lily on the glossy mahogany, I remained seated in my chair.

Agatha III

I drew several breaths deep down into my lungs, wagged my head from side to side and shrugged my shoulders to get the blood pumping. I often got cramp in the left side of my body. It was the one that faced the window.

Then I opened the door.

'Good day, Agatha, come on in.'

She seemed a little out of breath; she often turned up at the last moment and barely had time to take a seat in the waiting room before I called her in.

'Thank you, Doctor.'

After hanging up her jacket and disentwining

herself from a large knitted scarf, she lay down on the couch. Today she wore a purple dress and black ballerina flats, and her dark hair hung loose over her shoulders. Her short fringe made her look younger than she was, and as she lay there on the couch with her hands folded across her stomach she reminded me of a little girl from a fairy-tale I'd once read.

A few weeks earlier I'd asked her to note down all her dreams, and she started to tell me about the most recent one without my prompting: 'A man I didn't know wanted me to look through a telescope he had. At first the image was unclear, but when I adjusted the lens it came into focus. It was guts, lungs, heart, all kinds of organs. The telescope was inside me, you see.'

She hadn't made much mention of her family during the hours we'd spent together, but my sense that we were nearly there was swiftly confirmed.

'What do you think of when I say the word telescope?' I asked.

'My father.'

'And why's that?'

'My father was blind. He was so deft with his hands he could repair clocks and make things work even though he'd never seen what they looked like.

He had a little workshop where people came to him with devices that were broken, and they told him what they looked like and what they were supposed to do. Then he sat down with all his bowls and boxes of spare parts, and depending how complicated the mechanism was it would take him days or weeks to fix. But then it worked perfectly again.'

She smiled a kind of down-turned smile. 'Once he had a watch delivered from a woman who came from Switzerland. A very fine gold pocket watch. It had stopped after twenty years, and it took him five weeks before it worked again. The parts were so small I could scarcely pick them up with my fingers, but he had these small, tweezer-like . . .' Her voice faded.

'And the telescope in the dream, is that a reference to his lack of sight?' I enquired.

'Not exactly, no. My parents waited a long time before they had me. They were afraid his handicap was heritable, and that I'd be blind as well, but eventually they spoke to a doctor who didn't think that would be the case. So my mother fell pregnant. They were so relieved when the doctors said my eyes worked perfectly, and my father gave me a telescope with an inscription as a christening present.'

'What did it say?'

'*Für Agatha, meinen Augapfel.*'

The curious sounds meant nothing to me, but the meticulous emphasis on every single letter, suited Agatha exactly. Her name sounded different in German, and I wondered whether she was sick of hearing it pronounced incorrectly all the time. *Agatha.* I felt like saying it aloud as she had just done, but bit my tongue.

'It means something along the lines of "my eye apple",' she explained.

'Or "the apple of my eye", perhaps,' I suggested, then remarked, 'And now, in this office, you are turning the telescope on yourself.'

At that same moment it finally struck me what her fragrance was. Apples baked in the oven with cinnamon, the way my mother used to make them.

Between us

The day's count was five hundred and twenty-nine, and I woke at 6.25 a.m. with my heart hammering and a vehement tingling in my left leg. I thought at first I must have slept awkwardly, but it didn't stop when I took a walk around the front room. There's not enough space, I thought irritably as my hip bumped against the dining table, and what if I fell over in here? How long would it be before anybody found me? I felt a keen urge to take my pulse, but I knew it would only make matters worse, so instead I reassured myself that if I died of a heart attack on the spot then at least the whole thing would be over and done with. In which case it was irrelevant whether I was found or not.

It helped, and half an hour later I was shutting the door behind me. My briefcase in one hand and my stick in the other, I walked around the corner, crossed the Rue Martin and continued down the slope. The road seemed steeper than it had just five years earlier. It's things like that you don't find out until you're old: pavements are uneven, slabs are crooked, and you should have appreciated your legs more while they were still operational.

That day I took a little detour past a café I'd been using as the backdrop to a special fantasy for years. It had started when I happened to catch sight of a middle-aged couple sitting at one of the small tables inside. For some reason I paused in the street and stared as she lifted her hand to stroke his cheek. He leant into her palm, and – for all the world as though it were me sitting there – I felt the warmth of her flow over into him, making it impossible to know which one was which.

It had become a habit ever since to drop by the café and imagine that one day it might be me sitting there.

Today there were only a few people with newspapers

and morning coffee, and after a single searching glance I turned towards the clinic.

As I arrived Madame Surrugue rose from her desk to greet me. But our timing was off; I passed her the coat, she reached for the stick, and as I went to give it to her our hands collided. It was peculiar, for each moment had been pared down over the years to the barest necessities, and normally the whole thing flowed without either of us giving it a thought. I avoided her eye, feeling rather awkward and keen to reach the safety of my office. I accepted the stack of case files with a sound that might have denoted thanks, and fled.

Thankfully, the second I sank into the chair I forgot all about Madame Surrugue. Flicking vaguely through my notes, I quickly fell into a reflective mood. Imagine if it turned out life outside these walls was just as pointless as life inside; it was certainly a possibility. How often had I listened to my patients complaining and been glad their lives weren't mine? How often had I turned up my nose at their routines or secretly jeered at their foolish concerns? It occurred to me that I'd been imagining my proper life, my reward for all the grind, was waiting for me when I retired. Yet, as I sat there, I couldn't for the life of me work out what that existence would contain that was worth looking forward to. Surely the only things I could reliably expect were fear and loneliness? How pathetic. I'm just like them, I thought, and went out to greet the day's first patient with a throbbing in my hip and sorrow flickering beneath my ribs.

Agatha IV

I'd treated a number of manic patients over the years, and they had been unstable, restless or even slightly psychotic – once I'd spoken to a man who gambled away his entire fortune in three manic days because he believed he had a God-given ability to pick the winning horse.

But Agatha was different. Although she was clearly struggling, she turned up faithfully to every single session, and my impression was mainly that she was unhappy. In fact I was beginning to wonder whether the diagnosis from Saint Stéphane was even correct, so one day I decided to ask her.

'Agatha, you brought your case notes when you came to me, and there's something I've been wondering about.'

'Really? I've been wondering quite a few things myself,' she said tartly. 'For example, I don't understand how it helps an unhappy person to be tied to a bed and have electric shocks sent through their brain.'

'Hm, no,' I confessed, since personally I'd never been very fond of electrotherapy or insulin shocks, 'but they do say it has a good effect in difficult cases.'

She shrugged.

'Well, it didn't do me any good.'

'What I'm wondering about,' I explained, 'is your diagnosis. I've been talking to you for over two months now, and you strike me primarily as a depressive. Do you still have manic episodes?'

Agatha lay still for a moment, thinking.

'I'm not sure what constitutes manic. But I do get these wild fits of rage, and occasionally I'm gripped by a certain energy, and then I can barely hold back from doing myself violence. The other day I did this.' She lifted back her fringe to reveal a small but deep gash on one temple.

'Cupboard,' she said.

'Stupid,' I replied, thinking the diagnosis might be right on the money after all.

'I'm so glad I'm paying you such a fearful sum to probe the deepest recesses of my mind, Doctor.'

'Touché,' I said, and couldn't help smiling.

Once she had gone I wondered whether I might be the bipolar one. For although I still told myself Agatha was a nuisance and that she never should have come, wasn't it also true that I had begun to enjoy our conversations? And wasn't it the case, if I was honest, that I neglected to air out the office on the days she'd been there, trying to preserve the scent of apples just a little longer?

28 April 1948

Good morning Monsieur

For personal reasons I am unfortunately obliged to stay home from work for a few weeks, perhaps longer. Today's case files are ready, and the rest are, as

you know, archived by year and surname
behind the desk. My sincerest
apologies!

A Surrugue

The letter

In the course of the thirty-five years Madame Surrugue had worked for me, she had called in sick twice. Once when her mother died, and again when a violent attack of pneumonia kept her bedridden for several weeks – so it was with a certain unease that I read her letter. What could have happened?

The spring sun shone insistently, and the air in the office was stuffy and close. I threw open a window and picked up the sheaf of case files. It was strangely empty in the large room without my secretary, for although we'd never reached an informal, let alone friendly footing, she was as important a part of my workplace as the couch or my leather armchair.

The day's consultations passed without any of my patients managing to surprise or interest me. First was neurotic Madame Olive, who cleaned all the tea sets in her house every single morning before the rest of the family got out of bed. Then Madame Mauresmo, who was treated so badly by her husband that she should have left him long ago, but instead transformed her anger into shame before she noticed it. And finally Monsieur Bertrand, who, it seemed, mainly needed someone to talk to. He'd originally come to me with chest pains, and although I still listened to his echoing heart every once in a while, our conversations now revolved primarily around his difficulties asserting himself with his children.

I was sitting in my chair in a trance-like state, listening for the gist of Monsieur Bertrand's narrative, when suddenly there was a crash from the reception area. Excusing myself to my patient, I hurried out to see what was going on. A vase of yellow flowers had overturned on Madame Surrugue's large desk, and papers lay spread across the floor – it took a moment before I realised what had happened. I'd forgotten all about the open window, of course, and now the wind had punished me for it. My patients must have waited in a draught, too, and once again I caught myself missing my secretary. I shut the window and did a rudimentary job of tidying up, then returned to my patient. We soon wrapped up the consultation.

'See you in a week, Doctor.'

Monsieur Bertrand said exactly those words every single time we concluded a session; indeed, perhaps everything at my age was repetition. Four hundred and forty-eight, I thought, attempting to cheer myself up. Just four hundred and forty-eight more times I'd have to talk to one of these people, whom by now I didn't even try to understand.

After the morning's parade I walked the brief stroll to Mon Goût. The owner, whose name I didn't know but whose pockmarked face I'd seen five days a week since the restaurant opened, nodded mutely in the direction of my table. Moments later he arrived with a large plate of creamy potatoes and glazed ham.

Mon Goût wasn't renowned for its high standards of service, but the dish of the day was usually good and my table was always available. As I drizzled parmesan over the potatoes and shovelled down my food, I entertained myself by remembering which dishes were represented by the different numbers on the menu. By the time the meal was over and I'd washed it down with the customary two glasses of water, I'd got twenty-three out of twenty-four right.

Agatha V

At last she arrived, short-winded and frantically ruddy, and I straightened in my chair. There was no reason to look older than I really was.

'Good day, Agatha, do come in.'

'Good day, Doctor,' she answered breathlessly, 'so sorry to be late!'

She hung up a beige coat I hadn't seen before on the peg and asked, 'Tell me, where has your secretary got to?'

'I'm afraid for the time being my secretary is unable to come into work.'

'I see. So you're alone as well.'

She smiled conspiratorially, and I rose to the bait: 'Are you alone then, Agatha?'

She shrugged, shifted back further onto the couch, then lay down carefully, as though fitting into a template I couldn't see.

'One way or another I am. There's something lonely about not living. About watching other people play while your own legs are broken.'

I knew that feeling all too well, but luckily I was sitting in the therapist's chair while she lay on the couch.

'Agatha, you often speak as though your life were already over, and you'd ruined everything for yourself. Yet each and every moment you have a chance to do something you can be proud of.'

It was hard not to feel disgusted with my own sham. What choices had I made that I could be proud of? What big plans did I have for my retirement?

Agatha shook her head.

'It's much too late to be accepted into a good college now, and even if I knew what I wanted I don't have the money. If I was really serious about the piano or the singing, I would have done something about it sooner. I'm far too old now, Doctor.'

I imagined I could almost see the hopelessness like a thick haze between us, and I shifted forwards in my chair to keep hold of her: 'It's not true that everything is too late, Agatha. I believe life consists of a long series of choices we need to make. And only when we refuse to accept that responsibility does it all stop mattering.'

I'd said some variation on that line hundreds, maybe even thousands of times, but as I didn't have any real, positive experience to animate the words, they remained a pure abstraction. Still, I hoped Agatha would be able to use them. She lay there with her scarred wrists, brittle and transparent as glass, and although I felt like a hypocrite my intentions were good enough. I really did want to help her, and in its own way that complicated everything.

'I do hear what you're saying, Doctor. Don't you think I've tried telling myself the same thing?'

'Sometimes it helps to hear it from someone else,' I ventured.

'Maybe. And I do think I'm trying, but life keeps escaping me. It's right there – so close I can almost smell it.' She was gazing dreamily into space. 'But I simply cannot work out how one gets inside.'

After she was gone, with nearly soundless steps and her striped umbrella hanging loosely from her hand, I puzzled over what she might have meant by living.

From an outside perspective that was exactly what she was doing. Her heart beat, she had been educated and built a home, so if Agatha wasn't living then who was?

I switched off the desk lamp and walked through the office, the rushing of ephemerality in my ears. It was hard to appreciate that I would soon be closing down one final time, and I tried to imagine the doctor who would take on the clinic after me. Some springy young chap full of pep and rapid-fire solutions, probably. Would it be he who continued Agatha's treatment? He that ended up making her well? I know it was egotistical, but I'd rather she remained ill than be cured by someone else.

I spent a long time putting the files back in their proper place: it comforted me. Then I sat down in Madame Surrugue's abandoned chair behind the typewriter. Outside, the light diminished.

The looking-glass

Although I did my best to ignore it, there was no getting around the fact: my anxiety was getting worse. It happened more and more often that I woke with my heart hammering and the sense that death was at my heels, and naturally this rubbed off on my work. I began to doubt myself, and interpretations I'd put forward time after time stuck to the roof of my mouth, so I had to spit them out with such miserable timing it was a miracle nobody protested. But my patients were too well-brought-up, too self-absorbed, and by the time the last visitor of the week finally shut the door behind him I was fed up to the back teeth with the whole masquerade. Not even the day's count consoled me. If only somebody would put their foot down and ask me what the hell we were playing at, I thought, banging the door of the records cabinet so hard the key fell to the ground. It was a good thing Madame Surrugue wasn't there to see how I was treating her beloved furniture.

I took a breath, held it, then exhaled heavily.

My hands shook faintly, and the voices of my patients buzzed inside my skull, gathering at the temples into a collective, plaintive cacophony. Were all people really this miserable, or did I just see the unhappy ones? Was there anybody in those small homes outside who went to bed satisfied and knew why they were getting up again the next day?

It occurred to me that I'd forgotten to eat lunch.

I had no idea where the time had gone, and was briefly conscience-stricken at having made my scarred landlord wait in vain. Then nausea set in, and I had to force my legs to carry me to the little toilet, where I drank a few slurps of cold water straight from the tap. Sweat had gathered like an extra membrane over my back, and my heart was beating double time.

I shut off the jet of water and straightened up. The familiar tug of light-headedness swept through my body, and I gripped the sink so I didn't lose my balance.

When I stared into the mirror, looking for my face, it was empty.

There was no one there! And even though I knew perfectly well that we didn't have a mirror in that toilet, it took me long enough to remember that fact that the thought had time to form: *That's exactly how it is!*

I stood there resting against the cold porcelain sink until I was sure I could walk without falling. Then I pulled the chain, opened the door and left the room, glancing one last time over my shoulder at the bare white wall.

Tchaikovsky

After my experience I just wanted to go home, so I left the rest of the files where they lay and picked up my hat and coat without putting them on. The walk through the winding streets took nine and a half minutes on a good day, when my knees didn't hurt too badly, and even less today, when I was nearly jogging. Along the way I tried to convince myself I was somebody. That may sound like a bizarre project, but a man can indeed come to doubt who he is. I had neither family nor friends left – it's probably the norm to be in touch with people if they're going to count – and apart from an uncultivated interest in classical music I had no particular penchants besides drinking good tea and doing my job in an orderly manner. And even as far as that went, things seemed to be skidding downhill.

In a large, well-kept house with vine-covered walls an enormous woman sat in her front room, a television set lighting up her waxen face. Was I too going to spend the rest of my days goggling at a contraption like that, watching images of people I didn't know, planting flowerbeds in the garden, or just sleeping and eating while my body crumbled between my fingers? To make matters worse, I suddenly remembered an article I'd read recently about the surprising number of men who died just as they entered retirement and were about to enjoy all the time they finally had on their hands. Though that would at least solve the problem of working out what to do with myself, I thought darkly, pushing open the garden gate. When I entered the house I went straight to look in the refrigerator, but it was a depressing sight. A carton with two eggs, a jar of jam, some butter and a dry piece of cheese. I decided it was one of those days where I couldn't be bothered to boil eggs, so I made tea and some sandwiches, which I ate at the kitchen table to the sound of the heavily ticking clock. The bread was chewy, but if I'd been eating for pleasure the menu would have looked rather different.

Later I sat in my chair with the rug over my knees and let the hours pass me by, listening to music and reflexively setting the gramophone needle back to the beginning. My hand moved of its own accord, so that resetting the needle became part of the work, a setting back of time that simultaneously shifted it forwards with the same one gesture.

Eventually I needed to use the toilet, and as I stood there it occurred to me that I didn't even masturbate any more. How long had it been? I looked down and gave my neglected member a reassuring squeeze before zipping up and withdrawing. Then I put on my threadbare blue pyjamas and went to bed.

Agatha VI

One Saturday afternoon I was walking down the Rue du Pavillon on my way home from the weekly shop. On the corner, where the street crosses the Boulevard des Reines, I walked past the little café as usual, and when I looked inside I saw her: Agatha.

But it was another Agatha from the one I knew. She wore a dark red blouse that made her white skin glow, and although she was sitting down her whole body was in motion. Her hands drew great circles in the air, and her eyes shone darkly beneath her fringe as she explained something to the three other women at the table. Most beautiful of all was her mouth, when she threw back her head in almost uncontrollable laughter.

Without stopping to think I positioned myself behind a tree in a little garden diagonally across from the café, from which vantage point I could see the red dot that was Agatha. I tried to imagine what she would look like if it were us two sitting opposite each other at the table. More serious than what I'd just witnessed, but with the same soft mouth, I thought, while in my mind's eye I watched her brush back a few strands of hair from her face and lean forwards to put a hand on my forearm.

I stood there like some sleazy voyeur until Agatha emerged from the café and said goodbye to her friends. My knees were in agony, standing up for so long, but I scarcely noticed them, and when she started walking home through the city I followed. Walking with my shopping bags, I was intoxicated with a growing sense of desire and heavy with an all-too-familiar shame, until I saw her let herself into a whitewashed two-storey house on the Rue de l'Ancienne. A light came on in the front room. It felt strangely intimate to know that she slept in this building, that she bathed and dressed here, and that she walked on exactly this pavement every time she came to meet me.

I stood there for a while and pretended to search for something in one of the bags. Lifting a packet of finely cut ham, shifting a carton of eggs. My pulse throbbed in my burning cheeks, and it was an effort to breathe evenly. Then, pulling myself together, I walked swiftly past her house, turning my head at exactly the right moment to catch a glimpse inside. I don't know what I hoped to see, but she was seated in profile on the edge of a chair, staring into space, perhaps four metres away from me. Her face was a lifeless mask, and not until I squinted did I see the tears falling like drops of ink onto the red fabric of the blouse.

Excitement still resonated inside me like a piquant aftershock as I closed the door of my apartment behind me. It felt as though I'd uncovered a secret I longed to share with someone else; as though I'd been given a wonderful yet forbidden gift. My body thrummed, and again and again I saw Agatha in my mind's eye, the blouse against her slender body. For a moment I surrendered to enjoyment.

Then I opened my eyes again. It was impossible. Agatha was my patient, I was her doctor, and my job was to help her! Resolutely I grabbed my coat and hurried back out into the dusk.

The air down by the lake was like a badly needed cold shower, and by the time I'd done one lap the excitement was gone. Weariness caught up with me, and I limped the final stretch home with the image of a tearful Agatha seared onto my retinas.

The deaf, the mute
and the blind

Afternoon was becoming evening and two hundred and seventy-five patients had dwindled to two hundred and sixty-six when I finally emerged from the clinic a few days later. The sun hung low above the roofs, and the only sound besides the regular tapping of my stick against the ground was birdsong. Now and again a surname on one of the post boxes caught my eye as I passed, but it was rarely anyone I recognised. Given how many of the city's denizens I'd spoken to over the years it was rather astonishing how few I met outside the office. Sometimes it occurred to me I might

68

have fabricated the lot of them; even Madame Surrugue had, in a way, only stepped out of the clinic and into reality when she reported in sick.

The final slope was always the hardest, and I was glad when I reached No. 9. My hand had fished the key out of my coat pocket of its own accord when, out of the corner of my eye, I noticed a movement. It was my neighbour, and I was gripped by a diabolical urge to chase him out of the shadows. In an attempt to make him a flesh-and-blood human being I raised my hat and shouted, 'Good evening, neighbour!'

He stood in profile and didn't react to my greeting. He just opened the post box, took out a letter and closed it again. Only as he turned to walk back into his garden did he look up and catch sight of me. He nodded politely, and I tried again: 'Good evening, neighbour.'

He smiled and nodded once more, and on a sudden impulse I took a step forwards and said, 'It's amusing, really, that two people can live so close to each other, their lives only separated by a wall, and know so little about each other, don't you think?'

The man shrugged apologetically, pointing first at his ears then at his mouth, and shook his head.

Something inside me dropped. I felt a jolt in my belly, and my legs grew weak beneath me. The man was deaf. He had no idea I existed.

Abruptly I whirled around and rushed up the garden path and through my front door, banging it roughly behind me. Pressure built behind my eyes, and I collapsed onto a chair in the kitchen. Only much later did I realise I still had the stick in my hand and my overcoat on.

The visit

Gravity pulled the corners of my mouth towards the floor as I gathered the case files into a pile of drawings and randomly scrawled-down words and hobbled into the waiting room. I was picturing my skin being stretched further and further downwards until my cheeks hit the carpet with two tired slaps, and I had walked right up to the big table before I saw her. Like a vague reproduction of the woman who had once reigned from the self-same chair, she sat underneath the window. I paused in front of her, my arms still full of files, unsure of what to do next.

Finally I stretched out a hand towards her shoulder and cleared my throat.

'What are you doing here?'

My voice was much too coarse, much too loud, but she didn't seem to heed me at all; it was as though she were speaking to herself when, without looking at me, she said, 'Thirty-three days he's been home now, and he's so ill. He's dying before my eyes.'

Evidently I wasn't the only one keeping a count.

'Is Monsieur Surrugue unwell?' I enquired cautiously.

She looked up at me at last with an expression I'd never seen before, and blurted, 'I can't stand it any longer! And the worst thing is we can't even talk about it.' Her voice quivered. 'Thomas is petrified, I can see that, but he won't say anything. Usually we can talk about everything!'

'I'm sorry to hear that, Madame,' I said, hating myself for my inadequacy. 'You must let me know if there's anything I can do for you.'

These empty words were evidently all the encouragement she needed.

'Would you talk to him, perhaps?' she asked urgently.

I shook my head in confusion.

'But, Madame, how would that help?'

'I think it would do him good to speak to someone, but we're not religious, and he doesn't like his own doctor.'

'No, but—'

She cut me short: 'I don't sleep at night because I'm so afraid he'll be gone when I wake. I couldn't bear it if he died like that. I've put my mattress in his room, and I lie there all night listening while he breathes.'

'Madame, please,' I tried again, and what I really wanted to say was that I hadn't the least idea how to talk to another human being outside the four walls of my office. It was so long since I'd had a normal conversation with anybody that it hurt to think about it. I was helpless, in other words, and it struck me as ridiculous that she should turn to me in a situation such as this. Yet it was clear what was expected of me.

'Of course I'll speak to Thomas,' I said. 'I'll drop by some time over the next few days.'

'Oh, thank you so much, Monsieur!' The tense muscles in her face relaxed, and for a moment she took my hand between her own.

After Madame Surrugue left I was overcome by a fit of unease. I stood for a long time in the bathroom, my forehead against the cold wall, letting the water run over my hands. Breathing slowly, concentrating on keeping all thought at bay and coaxing my body into stillness.

What I most wanted was to turn my back on the whole thing, to crawl back into my usual rut, forget all about the dying man and simply count: 231, 230, 229. But even I realised that was impossible. A person I was fond of in my own bungled way was asking for my help. If I didn't at least try, then what was I good for?

Astray

That night I lay awake for ages in the bedroom, only the angular contours of the wardrobe and the glow from the window visible. At first I thought about Madame Surrugue, anxiously listening to her husband's breathing, and about what she imagined I might do for him. Then, as the chatter of the birds in the garden grew in strength, I began to wonder whether I would fight back on the day death came to take me.

By the time the alarm clock rang I had been reduced to a series of clumsily executed routines. I got up, heated water for the tea and took the milk out of the refrigerator as I usually did, but the unease wouldn't go away. Still, I ate a bit of bread and took an unusually long bath before fetching a clean shirt out of the pile of identical shirts from Le Tailleur. Then, exhausted, I set off to my steadily more slipshod clinic.

The sessions were hard to get through. Madame Brié's story about her mother's barely concealed indifference nearly made me well up, and I sniffled and coughed so many times she finally asked if I was coming down with a cold. Disquiet and something much akin to sorrow collected in my chest, and I began to doubt whether I could last a whole day of compressed human suffering. Before she left, Madame Brié shook hands with me and said, 'You can end up a very small creature if nobody cares about you. Sometimes I wonder whether such a creature is even a person at all.'

My next patient, eighteen-year-old Sylvie, was a no-show. It was rare that patients missed a session, but strictly speaking I couldn't know whether she'd tried to cancel, since I didn't have a secretary to take the message. Given the trials of the first few hours I ought to have breathed a sigh of relief, but instead I grew almost panicky: the cancellation forced me back into myself when all I wanted was escape. A cloud of confusing thoughts battled for space in my head. What would Madame Surrugue say when I tried talking to her husband and it became clear it wasn't working? How do you help a stranger to a good death when you can't even work out how to live your own life?

To interrupt my thoughts I got up and marched out into the reception area. There I wandered restlessly to and fro, adjusting a few magazines, gazing out of the window onto one of the square planes of grass, crossing over to the main door and peering down the street to see whether my patient was on her way. But there was no Sylvie, and there was no peace, and I was feeling worse and worse. My skin tautened around me like a net. I opened and closed my mouth, rolled my shoulders and straightened my spine, but there simply wasn't room enough in my body. Beside myself, I grabbed my stick and bolted out into the sunshine. I didn't know where I was going, only that I couldn't stay where I was, so I turned left and strode briskly down the street. Seeing nothing, I laboured down the road, inhaling in gulps. Confusing images came and went: Agatha's soft skin against the green fabric of the couch, myself alone at home by the window,

Madame Surrugue and her husband Thomas with their arms around each other. Occasionally I passed strollers on the pavement who had to jerk back so they didn't bump into me, but I barely heeded them. I was too focused on keeping myself upright, and when at last I collapsed onto the road I didn't know any more where I was.

As I gradually caught my breath, I realised I must have dropped my stick. I glanced around, bewildered. I was sitting on a raised flagstone border that screened a well-kept front garden from the road, and after taking a few minutes to recover I rose carefully to my feet, supporting myself on the cold stone. My body still worked, although my legs trembled beneath me, and I was drained of energy. As I teetered slowly down the street my vision began to expand once more, letting the world back in. What a blockhead, I scolded myself; why are you getting all het up? At the same time I knew that exactly the same thing might happen again tomorrow, and I'd be helpless to prevent it.

At the end of the road I found my stick, and soon afterwards I finally recognised a street. From there I hobbled back to the clinic. Even more distant than normal and with a rumbling belly, I made it through the last three consultations of the day. I sat, doddering and exhausted in my chair, while my shirt stiffened on my body like papier-mâché. My only words were good day and goodbye.

Once frightened Madame Mauresmo had, as usual, opened and shut the door behind her three times, marking close of day, I exhaled properly for the first time in hours. The nausea had been waiting for me, sloshing and astringent, and to my immense frustration I had to lurch outside to the toilet and vomit.

Agatha VII

'I think I was angry. No, I know I was; back then I just didn't dare feel it. But I stopped singing, I hardly ever touched the piano again, and that was when I started cutting my forearms.'

From my chair behind her I could make out the soft roundness of her cheeks, see the fine network of wrinkles around her eyes tighten.

'I don't know why I'm saying it like that. What's your opinion, Doctor – can one replace the piano with a paring knife?'

Laughter moved furtively in her voice.

'Mm, well, why not?' I replied. 'Just think of all

the art that's been produced through suffering and sublimation.'

She wore a bottle-green frock and some type of grey blouse on top of it. Dark shoes with a small heel, which jutted a fraction over the edge of the couch. Her feet tilted back and forth – first one way, then the other.

'Anyway, that was how it started. Ever since then I've cut myself, pulled out my hair, hit myself with different things and banged my head against the wall until it bled. And I can assure you it works better than ether and sleeping pills!'

'That may be so, but it works by drowning out the pain, not by removing it. You can't pretend you're actually solving anything by banging your head against the wall, Agatha, you're just punishing yourself for something you didn't do.'

It annoyed me that I sounded so old, and when her smile widened I was sure it was in amusement at me.

'No, Doctor,' she said. 'You're right. So you would suggest I stop? How original.'

'Tell me, is this a joke to you?' I blurted out.

'I can promise you it isn't,' she answered sharply. 'I'm buried alive in my own existence! One would think you could see through the gallows humour of a condemned woman.'

I leant towards her: 'But what is it you did so wrong, Agatha? Why are you so angry with yourself?'

She clicked her tongue. 'Have you even been listening, Doctor?'

'Yes, I believe so. But indulge me – explain it so I understand it.'

She exhaled audibly through her fringe, blowing it upwards. Her voice was back to its normal cadence as she replied: 'I'm angry because I haven't accomplished anything. I should have been someone, and I'm nothing.' For the first time during our sessions, the moisture in her eyes coalesced into a tear, which ran along her temple and continued down her white throat. I had to focus intently to keep track of the conversation, so that I didn't intermingle all my images of Agatha.

'I apologise if this is banal. I'm sure you've heard it before. But I really thought I was something special,' she said.

'And you still do, at least in part,' I replied. 'Or you wouldn't be so angry. Yet at the same time?'

'What do you mean?' She sniffed, whisking away the tear with the back of her hand.

'I mean you feel utterly unique and completely irrelevant at the same time.'

She nodded slowly. 'I think you're right there. One moment I don't think I deserve to live, and the next there's no one to match me. Silly, isn't it?'

Where death is

At last I couldn't put it off any longer. The past day or two's malaise gave way to a sense of unreality as I approached the house. What had I got myself into?

It took a while before Madame Surrugue answered the door.

'Good evening, Monsieur. It's very kind of you to visit. Do come inside,' she said, opening the door wide and stepping aside. Her face had come apart and been pieced back together in perfunctory fashion, and the sight made me want to swivel on my heel, bolt back down the garden path and vault onto the sweat-rank bus on which I'd arrived. Instead I stepped across the threshold, nearly tripping over an object that looked like a loom. I bit back an exclamation of surprise. There were things everywhere!

'Here, let me.'

Madame Surrugue put my stick in a stand that held at least ten umbrellas in various shades and draped my coat over a stack of newspapers, while I, flummoxed, tried to find a place for my hat. Never had I seen so many pairs of shoes, pitchers, fishing rods or, for that matter, watering cans gathered in a single home.

'This way,' said Madame Surrugue, leading me down a narrow hall.

'I think he's awake already, but if not it's fine to wake him.' She paused outside what had to be the sickroom.

I nodded.

'I'll be down here if you need anything,' said Madame Surrugue, continuing down the hallway.

'Wait,' I cried after her. 'What's wrong with him?'

She turned, looked me straight in the eye and said, 'He's got cancer.'

Then she vanished into the kitchen, and left me outside the door where death was keeping.

I knocked cautiously and entered. He was lying

in a double bed in the middle of the room, only his face protruding above the edge of the quilt. A deep furrow was chiselled between his overgrown brows, but as I approached this tormented expression was replaced by a friendly smile.

'Good evening, Doctor, do come in.'

There was an armchair in the corner, and I heaved it over to the head of the bed. The seat was low and eventually I just had to let go and permit myself to fall. One day, I thought, I'll simply stay wherever I happen to sit down, and I'll never get up again. In my chair by the window back home, maybe, or on a bench by the lake while the swans fall asleep around me.

'How are you feeling today, Monsieur Surrugue?' I asked.

'Thank you, I've been better,' he replied, 'but it was good of you to come. I believe my dear wife is running out of patience with me.'

The sunken head on the white pillow, the stench of illness lurking immediately beneath the scent of clean bedclothes. I said nothing, because I didn't know what.

He cleared his throat and continued: 'Do call me Thomas, Doctor. I won't mince words, now, although we don't know each other very well. I'm a burden to my wife, and I don't want to lumber her with my fear. But the truth is I'm terrified.'

He spoke haltingly, gathering a mouthful of air and delivering a sentence, inhaling again and delivering another one.

'I'm sure you're not a burden,' I tried. But Thomas didn't answer, and the silence was nearly impossible to abide. I knew it, I thought; I'm dreadful at this!

Then, from the pillow: 'Do you know death?'

I wrinkled my forehead.

'Don't we all?' I tried, but I could hear how hollow it sounded.

'I've spoken to many patients over the years who have been seriously ill or close to someone who's passed away,' I tried again, but that was almost worse. Finally I shook my head. 'No,' I said. 'I don't know death.'

Thomas smiled and nodded a few times.

'No, you see, one doesn't know it before it's there. Not really.'

His jaws moved beneath his stubble and his grey skin as though he were chewing. For a moment I wondered how quickly I might come to resemble him. There were still dark speckles in my grey hair, but that wouldn't last long if I became seriously ill. Ten kilograms of mixed muscle and fat were easily lost.

'Every night I lie here listening to my wife's breathing, and I think about how I'm ever going to be able to leave her.'

On the floor to his right, a mattress was made up with pillows and a duvet. On the bedside table to his left, where I was sitting, was a lamp, a glass of water, a basin and a tin of peppermint sweets. These, then, were death's remedies.

'To be honest, I'm not sure how I can help you, Thomas,' I said. 'I've never loved anybody.'

The words caught me off guard, but Thomas merely answered, 'No, we're not all that lucky. You might have an easier time with death.'

'Maybe,' I conceded, 'but a harder time with life.'

His laughter was stone falling on stone.

'You might have a point there,' he spluttered, the laughter turning into a cough. 'A life without love isn't up to much.'

I smiled back at him, and we sat for a while in silence before I asked, 'You said you were afraid?'

'Absolutely scared witless!' He smiled again, this time with his eyes. 'Feels nice to say it out loud.'

'I'm afraid too, you know,' I confessed. 'I just haven't worked out why.'

'I think the worst thing is not seeing my wife's face again. Having to go somewhere she isn't.'

Somehow I understood precisely what he meant.

'Maybe she's not the one you have to let go of,' I suggested. 'Maybe it's just everything else?'

I wasn't sure if that made sense, but Thomas reached out and took my hand in the same way his wife had done a few days earlier.

'That's true.' I felt his grip tighten, the weak pressure. 'Her I can never let go of. But the rest of it, perhaps.'

He relaxed his grip, doubling up into another dry fit of coughing. I passed him the water and he drank a few sips.

'I hope you find out what you're afraid of,' he said hoarsely, reclining back against his pillows. 'Anything else would be a frightful waste.'

I looked down at him and shrugged; hadn't it been a waste so far, most of it? Still, I asked: 'How do you work out what you're afraid of?'

'In my experience,' answered Thomas as his eyes drifted shut, 'you start with your greatest longing.'

Agatha VIII

'People said I looked like my father, and he loved that. I think he was proud of having produced a child despite his handicap, so I became a kind of trophy. Play, Agatha, play!'

The words were a sneer.

'You were talented?' I asked. Of course she was.

'They never told me I was good, I just heard them saying so to other people when they thought I wasn't listening. But yes, I was very talented.'

'And that didn't make you happy?' I looked at her slender fingers, imagining them chasing over the keys as though she wanted to force herself into a mistake.

Suddenly I remembered the day I'd realised I only played the violin for my father's sake. That I practised exclusively to avoid his disappointment, and that all I felt when a piece went well was relief.

Agatha shook her head.

'No, I hated it. I hated the piano, and I hated hearing them talk about me. It was all about showing other people what good parents they were. It had nothing to do with me.'

Strictly speaking the session was over, but I didn't have the heart to cut her off, and what I really wanted was to stay here with Agatha and make the next patient wait. To look at her white skin and imagine how it would feel against my palm; to ask a question and know that I could make her well if I used the right words.

Yet she must have sensed a shift, because although I neither moved nor spoke she sat resolutely upright. Her hair was dishevelled and damp, like that of a child woken from a deep sleep.

'I think that's all for today, Doctor. I'll see you on Tuesday.'

She shot me a smile that looked more like a rehearsed grimace, and I nodded.

'Let's say that, then, Agatha. It's been a pleasure.'

Her hand rested in mine for a moment, then she let herself out of the office. I sat on the couch, which was warm from her body, and drew a long, pleasurable breath. Then I called Madame Carmeille inside and tried to convince myself she was just as important.

Snow

One day I woke up to a thin white membrane over the city. I have always loved winter with its muted sounds, and would take snow rather than sunshine any day of the week. This time it came unexpectedly, just as spring was verging into summer, and that only made me appreciate it all the more.

The snow revealed a secret world of footprints: dogs' paws, boots and tiny children's feet, which turned off towards the school or continued past the clinic and onwards in the direction of the city centre.

In the office, where dust and dead flies accumulated on the windowsills, I did the first sessions of the day. In my heart of hearts I cursed all the things afflicting my patients, about which there was nothing I could do. There were emotionally frigid marriages and wine bottles behind the bookcase to contend with, and how much could really be expected of therapy when I only had a few hours a week to build up what my patients had spent a whole lifetime tearing down?

Then Madame Almeida arrived. She began to talk the second her head hit the cushion, and I wondered whether she would notice if I quietly died of boredom in the chair behind her. To think that Madame Surrugue was about to lose her husband, and this appalling female was obsessed with whether she'd been cheated out of ten centimes when she bought gloves!

The thought sent a tart reproof up my throat and over my patient: 'Madame, this has got to stop,' I interrupted. It happens sometimes that a man surprises himself, and this was one of those times.

'Every time you come you spend the whole time telling me how other people are good-for-nothing, and it's driving me out of my wits! Nearly three years now you've been complaining about your lazy husband and ignoring absolutely everything I have to say. It ends here!'

Madame Almeida levered herself up awkwardly on her elbows and fixed me with a look of disbelief. The loose skin underneath her chin was quivering faintly, and her eyes were wide.

'I think we should run an experiment, Madame. You're clearly not getting much benefit by coming here, so I suggest trying something new. Until next week, when we see each other again, I want you to avoid all agitation. You must tell your husband that he's in charge of practical matters, because you've been given orders to rest, and then I just want you to enjoy the weather, read a book, or do whatever else you feel like. Spend time with some good friends.'

Madame Almeida spluttered, purplish-red in the face: 'But Bernard can't cook! He can't do laundry or iron; Bernard can't do *anything*!'

I shrugged. I didn't give a fig about Bernard.

'We can't know that until he's given a chance,' I said, with as much kindness as I could muster. 'It's just an experiment, and there's no bad outcome. Simply do your best and we'll take stock next time.'

Madame Almeida stared at me for another few seconds. She looked like she was trying to formulate something but couldn't find the words, because reality had slipped out of her grasp. I rose to indicate that the conversation was at an end, and she followed me mechanically to the door.

'Well, I never heard the like in all my days, Doctor,' she finally managed to say, and I had to suppress a smile.

'I think we need a change, Madame. Wouldn't you agree?'

She shot me a final mistrustful glance, clutched her bag hard against her chest as though I'd tried to steal something from her, and left the office with short mincing steps in her elongated skirt.

After she was gone I wondered whether I might never see her again, but I doubted it. She needed witnesses to her martyrdom, or else there was no point. And if she didn't come here to grumble, where was she going to go?

The day was over, and all I had to do was close up the clinic. Then came the fear. My pulse vibrated in my body as though I were a tuning-fork in the hand of a furious composer, and if it hadn't happened many times before I would have been certain I was dying. I had to keep pausing on my way from the office to the waiting room, stopping at the patients' chairs and taking deep breaths, only to get up again a moment later because I couldn't bear being still.

My legs hummed beneath me, but finally I got Madame Almeida's file and the day's half-finished drawing back in place, then I set out into the early evening. Paper-thin blotches of snow still patchworked the roofs, while stretches of black and green appeared on the damp earth and the wind tore at my lungs.

Slowly the sweat dried on my skin. Gripping my stick firmly, I moved through the city, heading directly away from home, and I was a few metres from her house before I let myself realise what I'd done. If only I could catch a glimpse of her I'd feel better, of that I was sure. If only I could see she existed.

But Agatha wasn't there. Instead there was a thin man with high temples, sitting at the dining table and reading the newspaper. *Julian*. I felt a stab of revulsion; what on earth did she see in him? Why was she with a man who clearly didn't make her happy?

At that moment he looked up. For one protracted moment I gazed directly into his pale fish's eyes – which, truth be told, were probably just blue – before I tore myself away and hastened back through the city, filled with a mixture of humiliation and rage.

Agatha IX

'What are you so afraid of, Agatha?'

'Oh, I hardly know any more. What are we all afraid of?' She threw up her hands despairingly. 'I think life itself has become dangerous. I'm afraid of playing music, afraid of stopping, afraid of getting close to people, afraid of being alone. There's no place for me anywhere!'

'But you've got to try, Agatha,' I said. 'Life is made up of what we do, and you're not doing anything.'

She groaned and shifted irritably: 'But I won't cope if it all goes haywire again. So far it's done nothing but, it's unendurable!'

An unexpected wave of tenderness washed over me, and I had to resist the impulse to reach out my hand.

'But Agatha, what do you think life is?' I asked softly. 'What do you mean?'

'It seems to me you think there's some formula for the good life, and as long as you haven't found it you might as well stop living at all. Is that right?'

She sat bolt upright, side-on, her hands kneading the seat either side of her knees.

'I believe life is much too short and much too long all at once. Too short to learn how one ought to live. Too long because the decay only gets more and more visible with every passing day.'

Her voice was like a chant, and she was clearly distressed, but I couldn't let my weakness for her get in the way of the therapy.

'How do you know you're a failure?' I persisted.

She shook her head and murmured, 'Believe me, it's the kind of thing you notice.'

'And against whom are you measuring yourself?'

'Against the woman I should have been.' She rubbed her face harshly with both hands. 'I'm tired now, Doctor. We'll have to leave it there for today.'

Our eyes locked. She looked unhappy, or was I

reading myself into her? I imagined stretching out my hand to stroke her hair. Her leaning in towards me so I could hold her, until all distance vanished and I could whisper that I understood her. That I was at least as afraid as she.

Instead we said goodbye and she left me in the chair. I counted her steps through the room – she took nine where I took eight – and heard the outer door close behind her with a metallic snap.

Love

On the day I had two hundred and two sessions left to go, I awoke hot and blotchily red with the sheet and eiderdown pressed up against the wall in a sweaty clump. The countdown had pursued me through my dreams, where I ran to and fro in perplexity, trying to rescue all my patients before we came to die, and the sense of being rushed off my feet would not be shaken no matter how long I stood in the bath. It would all be over soon, and what then? Had I really done everything in my power to help them?

As I reached the clinic I paused for a moment in the doorway and gauged the room. Was there not a peculiar smell? A little as though I'd forgotten something in the refrigerator, something that had sunk into a damp puddle at the back, or hadn't emptied the bin? I rarely gave it much thought, but Madame Surrugue had used to clean up and change the towel in the bathroom, and she often bought flowers to arrange in vases about the place. Without her the clinic was slowly but surely disintegrating around my ears. The patients swapped places on the couch as though according to an intricate pattern somebody with the right perspective might be able to divine. I thought of Thomas. There had been a kind of openness between us when we met that I wished I could carry over into my sessions. Death had forced us, or so it felt, to skip a whole series of stages and go straight to the essentials, but could it not be done without death's intervention?

While Madame Olive mused on the notion of love, I continued to speculate. Perhaps it wasn't possible to build a genuine relationship here at the office, where one person was paying another to listen, and where the patients by definition were ill while I held the cure.

'I don't actually think it is love I feel for my husband,' I heard Madame Olive declare. 'Although we do often say we love one other. One says many things.'

'Mnh,' I murmured.

'On the other hand I'd rather be with him than be alone. That must mean something.'

I murmured again, wondering whether it meant anything other than that she was afraid to be alone.

'Maybe,' sighed Madame Olive, 'I wouldn't have to polish all the silverware every day if I only loved my husband a little more.'

I couldn't help but laugh at that: 'You mustn't say that, Madame. I think you should try to find a little more love for yourself.'

Madame Olive smiled, taken aback.

'I never looked at it like that before, Doctor.'

By 6 p.m. I'd spoken to four patients before lunch and four afterwards, but I wasn't tired. On the contrary, I felt like dancing, like tearing out my old bones and taking another chance as a young, virile man. Banal as it may sound, I wanted deeply to be a person who meant something to someone.

Oddly restless and unable to make up my mind to go home, I wandered aimlessly around the clinic. First along the walls in the big room, past Madame Surrugue's chair, where I let my fingers stroke the beautiful desk, then back to my own office. I really loved this place. It was here I'd first found something that was mine, and that I might even be good at. Why had I let it slip away? Was I just lazy, or was I genuinely so arrogant that I'd become bored by other people's misery?

Walking across to the window, I peered out over the deserted street. Felt the cool wood of the windowsill press against my palms, rocked a little back and forth. Then I leant all the way forward until my forehead touched the glass, and I could feel the blood throbbing where the skin rested against the pane.

The decision

It was 7.35 a.m., and the sky was an ice-blue field high above me. A group of children with freshly pressed school uniforms and slicked-down hair made playful lunges at each other, battling to see who could avoid being pushed onto the road. They must be on their way to the École de Saint Paul on the other side of the city, and a number of the mothers who had just kissed them goodbye were sure to have visited my couch over the years. Suddenly a bright childish voice immediately behind me cried out, 'Good morning, Monsieur!'

It was the little girl from No. 4. She almost danced

past me with a kind of tripping urchin's hop, and before I could reply she was already some way down the street, her schoolbag bobbing up and down on her back.

As soon as I glimpsed my practice at the bottom of the road, I knew Madame Surrugue had still not returned; the emptiness practically radiated from the brickwork. Solitude is total, I thought, unsure whether it was merely my own that I meant.

Once the day was over and I'd temporarily set the eight case files on the corner of my secretary's desk, a decision fell into place in my mind. The thought had perhaps germinated some time during the night, and now it made me stop at the florist, where the husband of one of my patients kindly helped me pick a bouquet of flowers whose names I didn't know, before I was escorted up the Rue du Pavillon and onto the crowded, reeking bus 31. On the way I recalled my first meeting with Madame Surrugue. She had replied to the job advertisement I'd put in the local paper once I realised I couldn't play doctor *and* handle all the administrative matters at the practice. I'd set aside a whole day for interviews, but after just the first three candidates I was ready to give up the idea of ever finding a person I could stand to work with.

Then she arrived. Impeccably dressed in a long skirt and matching jacket, her hair scraped back into a tight bun I'd never once seen her without. For some reason I also very clearly remembered her brown leather shoes, with a low, angular heel and a buckle at the front, which she wore for at least five years after she entered my employment.

I asked her to take dictation on the typewriter, which she did swiftly and faultlessly, before enquiring as to her previous places of work.

'I helped my father in his shop from the age of twelve, and I was the one who did the accounts and made fair copies of the letters he sent to suppliers and customers. At nineteen I got a job with a solicitor, and ever since then I've been responsible for his schedule, all his paperwork, archiving his files and so on.'

She handed me a neatly folded piece of paper, which contained some laudatory words about her efforts.

'By all means contact him to assure yourself of the quality of my work.'

The next day I informed Madame Surrugue, who

back then was Mademoiselle Binout, that the job was hers.

I didn't see the red house with the wrought-iron number 12 on the garden gate until the bus was driving past it, and I surprised myself by shouting loudly to the driver so I could get off. It was a relief to escape the mass of tightly sardined human bodies, and once outside I wiped my hands on my trousers almost frantically.

A few years after taking her on I contacted Monsieur Bonnevie, the lawyer Madame Surrugue had named as her former employer. I wanted to enquire about the possibility of buying the practice – which until then had only been leased to me – and was greatly astonished to find that when I praised our mutual secretary he said he'd never heard of her in his life. I never mentioned it to Madame Surrugue. Her work was irreproachable, and in any case I took a strange pleasure in having exposed her. It was a secret that was at once ours and mine alone, and her bluff had only made me respect her all the more.

'Good day, Madame.'

I bowed and lifted my hat, but I hadn't thought

the visit through properly, and suddenly I had no idea what to do with myself. Madame Surrugue was staring at me as though she'd forgotten who I was, and I cleared my throat uncertainly as I shifted my weight from one leg to the other. I was struck by how different she looked. She appeared to have lost several kilograms, and the dishevelled bun bristled with tufts of hair, streaked with a grey I'd never previously noticed.

Then I remembered the flowers still clenched in my clammy grip, and I handed them to Madame Surrugue as though passing her my stick. Perhaps she too fell into the old habit, because she took the bouquet, and it seemed to help her remember how to be human.

'Thank you so much, Monsieur. I'll put these in water straight away,' she said, stepping aside as she opened the door. 'Do come in, won't you?'

Coffee

'I've been hard-pressed to manage without you, as I'm sure you can imagine,' I began – a sentence I'd come up with on the bus. I described how the case files were piling up on her desk, and how many of the patients had asked after her and sent their best wishes.

'How thoughtful,' she smiled weakly. 'But I must say I don't understand how hard it could be to archive the files in the cabinet where, as you know, they've always been!'

It was nice to be rebuked, and Madame Surrugue's cheeks flushed slightly as she talked.

'I've been working for you for over thirty years, more or less without taking any holiday, and now the whole house of cards threatens to topple the moment one takes the liberty—'

She passed her hand swiftly across her mouth, and we sat for a few seconds in silence. Then she rose abruptly.

'Coffee?'

I watched her as she worked. Her movements were slower and somehow less efficient than at the clinic, and it made me at once sad and strangely honoured that I was allowed to see her this way.

'How kind of you to come and see us again,' she said, still with her back turned. 'Thomas greatly appreciated your last visit, and he has seemed calmer lately.'

'I'm glad to hear that,' I replied, shaking my head, 'but I think mostly he was the one who helped me. How is he doing today?'

'He's just fallen asleep,' she answered, putting the coffee pot on a tray. 'He had a bad night. There have been many of those.'

Coming over to the table with the tray, she nudged a few stacks of paper aside and placed the saucers, cups, sugar, cream jug and coffee in front of us.

'How long has it been going on, this?' I asked. Her movements controlled, Madame Surrugue smoothed the tablecloth in front of her a few times, then sighed.

'It started a while before I reported sick. Thomas had been getting stomach ache for several months, but he wouldn't go to the doctor. By the time we finally got around to going they said flat-out there was nothing to be done, so I might as well take him home again. And that was when I decided to stay here with him.' She looked up, her eyes shining. 'He could die at any time, really.' I nodded and looked down at her hand, which lay on the table in front of me. It looked like a bird somebody had flung down from the sky.

'Thomas is a good man,' I said, struck once again by how inadequate words can be. Madame Surrugue must have been married to Thomas for more than twenty years. Now he was dying just on the other side of the wall to my right, and all I could think of to say was that he was a good man.

But Madame Surrugue simply nodded, poured coffee for us both and put her feet up on the nearest chair.

'To think of it,' she said, almost wonderingly, as she studied me with narrowed eyes.

I shifted uneasily in my seat.

'To think of what, Madame?'

'Well, that you came,' she said, dropping her gaze as she blew on her coffee and took a sip. 'Just like that. I never would have believed it.'

I reached for my cup and smiled back.

'It's the least I could do,' I said.

Agatha X

She sat by the window with the fragile sun of early summer in her hair and the look of someone far away. If you didn't know better it would be impossible to tell she was ill. For a long moment I just stood there gazing at her, then I pulled myself together.

'Good afternoon, Agatha,' I said. 'Come in.'

'Thank you,' she replied, walking past me into the office. 'You look melancholy today, but of course you always do. Are you melancholy, Doctor?'

The question was simple, but nobody had ever asked it before, and it hit me like a punch to the gut.

'I . . .' I started, but suddenly my throat was much too dry, and I had to swallow before I could continue: 'I haven't given it much thought.'

'You haven't given it much thought?' She sat down on the edge of the couch and gazed at me challengingly. Her big eyes were far too close, and it was an effort to look away.

'No,' I said.

She wrinkled her brow: 'But Doctor, how can you spend your life alleviating the suffering of others without any regard for your own?'

Bloody heat. I would have given anything to open a window, but my legs felt sapped beneath me, so I remained in my chair while a burning warmth spread out from the centre of my chest.

'I've probably developed a certain ability to shrug off those questions when I leave the office in the evening,' I said in a tone of voice I hoped sounded laid-back. 'But how are *you* doing today, Agatha?'

'You don't want to answer?' she asked insistently. 'How can you claim to understand other people if you don't even know how *you* are?'

She held my gaze, and I sank further and further while the pencil, notepad and all the textbooks vanished, until finally I was left bare, a fearful man of almost seventy-two, with smeared glasses and stubble that was much too long.

It felt as though an incredibly long time passed before I answered. 'Well, I suppose I can't. You're right.' I threw up my arms. 'I have no idea what makes people tick! What do you say to that, then? The whole thing's a charade!'

Agatha exhaled through her nose, a cross between a snort and a laugh: 'All right, well, you're exaggerating, Doctor! I've spoken to lots of medical men before you, and vanishingly few of them actually listened to what I said. I very much appreciate your help.'

I understood nothing; hadn't we just agreed I was a fraud?

'Simply coming here and speaking to somebody who's actually interested in me and doesn't merely tell me I should be committed, that means a lot. Do you not realise that?'

I shook my head.

'Well it does. But it still makes no sense to me that you can sit here and profess to be an expert in mental disorders if you haven't even considered that you yourself might be struggling.'

Finally my voice returned: 'But what makes you think I'm struggling?'

'Where shall I start? You've been falling apart ever since your secretary got sick. There's a peculiar smell in here, the office is a shambles, and I get the feeling you've been wearing the same suit since the first day I met you.'

She revealed her pointed chin in a smile, but continued more seriously, 'Then there's your shaky hands, of course.' I glanced down in surprise at my liver-spotted hands. 'But it's your face that really gives you away. Even when you smile you're sad.'

Yes, well, I thought, she was probably right about that. But what was I supposed to do about it? It was life itself that had disappointed me.

'Why do you think I sit back here where no one can see me?' I asked, trying not to lose my grip entirely.

'Aha,' she pointed menacingly at me. 'It's all beginning to make sense now!'

I laughed in a voice that wasn't my own, or perhaps it was the laughter I didn't recognise. But there was something liberating about being seen by Agatha.

'Right, so you *can* actually laugh,' she said. 'That's annoying. Means I owe Julian lunch.'

Swimming

The fear had lain in wait. As soon as Agatha left the office it surged in over my feet. There were a terrifying number of hours still to go before I could lie down and sleep, and the mere thought of running from the fear for that long made me tired.

On the way home I bought bread and ham for dinner. The sales assistant was oddly blurred; I couldn't bring his features into focus, and my pulse roared in my ears.

'Ninety centimes, Monsieur.'

I handed him some money and turned to go.

'Monsieur, your change!' I heard from somewhere

behind me, but I was locked into a movement that could not be stopped.

There was a crackling in my chest, and I sensed rather than decided that my steps were taking me towards the lake instead of the direct route home. *Agatha, Agatha*, it sang in my head; suddenly there was water before my feet, and I didn't falter even when the chill crept through my shoes.

Another step. The ground was hard and yielding at the same time, the water lapped halfway up my shins, and never in my life had anything felt so soothing. The coldness percolated through my trousers, through my skin and deep into the heat of fear, and once the water reached my hips I let myself slip forwards and I dived, submerging the whole of my sweaty, taut-strung body.

'Aaaaah,' I sighed, flipping onto my back and swimming with a liberating ease I had forgotten existed, out into the middle of the lake.

Little things

The first patient of the day was no less than Madame Almeida, and I made a mental note that after her I would have precisely one hundred sessions left. The enormous woman had been absent from all our appointments since I'd caught her off guard with my experiment, and I'd started to think I might have misjudged her.

Yet, suddenly, there she was. Her mouth was a thin, bitter line, her heels clacked accusingly across the floor, and most strikingly of all she was silent.

'So, how have you been over the past few weeks, Madame?' I began.

She shrugged.

'Last time I gave you a difficult task. Perhaps you could tell me how you got on?'

She gave me a curt glance.

'It didn't work.'

'All right, but that's also a result,' I said encouragingly. 'In what way did it not work?'

'Well, it was impossible. It was completely idiotic!'

She looked up at me again like a truculent child, her bottom jaw protruding, and I had to stifle a grin.

'You simply don't know Bernard,' she continued. 'And I'm beginning to think you don't know me either!'

'No?'

'No! If you did you'd never have suggested I take any rest. The only way I can get any peace is when I'm busy.'

'Aha,' I smiled.

'Aha what?' she spat. 'All you do is sit there with your "mhm"s and your "aha"s, and what use is that to me?'

She might have a point there, but I wasn't going to let her wriggle out so easily today.

'Remind me again what it is you require help with, Madame?' I asked.

'Oh for heaven's sake, this is beyond a joke,' she spluttered. 'You're asking me that after three years?'

'I thought you came here to get your nerves under control. We've discussed everything from your childhood to your breathing to absolutely no avail, so the next logical step must be to turn our focus on the present, and on learning to take the small stuff a little less to heart. But you refuse to do so. So now I'm asking: What do you actually want my help with?'

Madame Almeida collapsed. Her broad shoulders lost breath, and her back curled protectively over her many-rolled belly.

'If you wish to get better, Madame, I see two options. They may even go hand in hand. One involves becoming less engrossed in all the day-to-day pettiness and cutting down on your regular duties. The other, finding something that gives your life meaning.'

She was listening, that much was clear. Perhaps she didn't yet understand what I was saying, but she was trying.

'What I mean is that you should start spending time on something that really means something to you, something bigger than shopping and cleaning. Something that makes you happy! Or,' I added hastily, 'at least something that interests you. Then all the little things will probably start to pale.'

'All the little things?' she asked, her head bowed and her bottom lip quaking.

'Yes,' I replied. 'All the things with which you so painstakingly pad out the hours, even though in reality they only make you angry. There's got to be something more than that!'

Madame Almeida sniffed. Then she nodded hesitantly and looked up at me.

'You know, it's funny you should say that, Doctor,' she remarked. 'I've always thought the same myself.'

Clearing out

That evening I suddenly found it hard to reconcile myself to the notion that my home looked exactly as it always did. I gazed around, and although everything was familiar, it felt simultaneously obtrusive and out of place. It struck me that never in my adult life had I acquired a single new household item: not so much as a fork or a new mattress for my bed.

Everything had been either inherited or given to me by my parents, and I kept it because it worked.

So I started with my father's pictures. One by one I lifted them down from their nails, and as I did so I grew steadily more astonished at how discoloured my walls really were.

There were seven pictures in total, all of which I remembered better than my father's own face when I shut my eyes. Several of them were older than I was; they had always hung there, and I had never stopped to consider whether I actually liked them. Then I turned to the bureau. I hadn't looked inside in many years, and it was with a certain curiosity that I combed through the drawers. My parents had not been sentimental folk – they had never, for instance, told the usual funny stories about things I'd done as a child. But in one of the drawers I found a box of my milk teeth, and in several of my father's paintings there were faint traces of someone I had always known was me. A child's compact footprint in the sand, a tall and a short figure among the trees in a forest far away.

In the bottom drawer I found a cloth, and I began piling onto it the things I intended to throw out. The top drawer was sticking, but I jerked it roughly open. It turned out to contain some of my father's art supplies: coloured chalks and oil paint, brushes neatly stowed in bags and a couple of full sketchbooks. I also found the tin of special pencils my father only let me use when we were drawing together.

The little drawers at the very top contained my parents' correspondence from the time before my mother moved from England, as well as some photographs, a letter-opener and a white paper bag of stamps that had long since gone out of production. Most of it went onto the rubbish heap, and then I reached for one of the black notebooks I had found, to my delight, in the middle drawer. I had used them years ago during late afternoons, once the final patient had shut the door behind them, and for want of better things to do I discussed the cases with myself. *Practise listening*, it said somewhere, and I felt a quiet prickle of regret at the thought of my younger self, sitting there puzzling over how to get better at his profession. I stroked my index finger across the eager markings on the paper. The writing was identical; the man had become someone else while I wasn't looking.

I sat for a long time in the same position and flicked through the notebooks, taking pleasure in good observations and reminiscing about particularly difficult or lovable patients, until finally I couldn't do it any more. Everything ached.

Wearily I sat down on the edge of the bed and wondered whether I could be bothered to brush my teeth. Instead I leant back until I was lying down, my legs still hanging off the edge and my feet resting on the floor. I woke like that in the middle of the night, agonising cricks everywhere, and I barely managed to take off my shoes and crawl beneath the covers before I fell back to sleep.

The next day I came round in a sore but wonderfully relaxed body. I ate breakfast in the front room, which looked new and bare without the paintings; like a canvas begging to be filled. When I left the house I was dragging a big bag, which I chucked onto a tip a few streets away.

12/5-1928, notebook no. 4

General remarks

It works well sitting behind the patients; they speak more freely and draw deeper connections. Read more about the interpretation of dreams; how ought Madame Tremblay's recurring dream about losing her teeth be understood?

My style

Trying to ask fewer questions, give the patient more space. Difference between open and closed questions; asking to understand, not to manipulate. Alain spoke about his sister, who drowned before his eyes. What does one do with one's own grief during therapy? Didn't want transference to become an issue, so I said nothing. Where is the line between coldness and professionalism?

Alain: Moving towards the heart of the trauma; loss of his sister, feeling of guilt and lack of affection from his mother. Continue.

Mme Tremblay: Could the teeth be read as loss of power? Helplessness in a bad marriage?

Mlle Sofie: Not very far along yet, she's skimming the surface. Must direct more actively.

M. Laurant: Very compulsive. Brings own blanket for the couch and washes in between each time. Anal fixation?

Mme Mineur: Very sweet. Maybe too sweet; never asserts her own will, lets me take the lead in everything – a reflection of her behaviour in the real world?

M. Riccetuer: Depression. Hardly speaks. What happened??

Agatha XI

Six sessions to get through before I reached hers. I'd played over our last conversation several times in my head, and in all honesty I didn't know what to expect. Could we go on as before, or had she somehow lost respect for me after my meltdown?

When I opened the door to call her in she was leaning against the wall, looking out of the window.

'I think summer has arrived without me noticing, Doctor,' she said, turning towards me. 'Only a few weeks ago it was snowing, and now everything's in colour.'

I glanced out onto the road. She was right; the

bushes had come to life in a flood of green, and the grass on the lawns was juicy and thick. By the time I blossomed into a pensioner it would be high summer.

I sat down behind Agatha and waited expectantly as she lay in silence for several minutes. When she finally spoke it sounded as though she had formed the words in her mouth much earlier and had carried them around until they could be released here: 'Do you remember the day you asked what I was afraid of, Doctor?'

'Yes?'

'You may already have guessed, but my father touched us. Mostly me – I was born first – but also Veronika. Sometimes he grabbed me as I walked past his chair, and I couldn't get away again. Then he'd start groping me, moving from my thighs up between my legs, around my hips and bottom, over my chest and up my neck. He finished with my face.'

She swallowed with difficulty, her voice flat and distant as she recited the path his hands had taken. Repugnance welled up inside my body as she spoke. She was right – I had sensed it might be the case, yet it still made me furious. I'd heard stories about abuse before, but this was more subtle, better masked.

'He always spent the most time on my face,

especially my mouth. I couldn't let myself cry, because then he'd comfort me, and that was almost worse.'

My jaw tensed at the thought of her father's gratified face with its wide, blind eyes and Agatha's rigid childish body beneath his hands. I realised I was squeezing the pencil so hard it hurt, and relaxed my grip.

'It was so disgusting,' continued Agatha. 'I hated it, but my mother said it was natural, it was just his way of seeing. That he was trying to understand who I was.'

'When did it stop?' I asked.

'It didn't really, I just left home. But it got easier to avoid, because when I finally went back to visit they usually had other guests as well. He died ten years ago.'

'And your mother?'

'She still lives there,' sighed Agatha. 'I visit her a few times a year, but often it . . .' – she searched for the word – 'well, we end up deadlocked.'

'It sounds as though your mother was just as blind as your father,' I said, hoping she wouldn't hear the tremor in my voice. If I'd been able, I would have beaten the living daylights out of both her parents.

'Actually I think my mother knew perfectly well

what he was doing,' she replied. 'But I can't work out if she didn't care or if she actively liked seeing me suffer.'

I was struck by a sudden thought.

'Agatha, do you remember the telescope from your dream?'

'Yes?'

'Can you see what it was we didn't understand back then?' I leant towards her in excitement.

She hesitated: 'No . . . what do you mean?'

'I mean that the telescope is your fundamental conflict!'

I was nearly shouting now, but I was too eager to stop: 'More than anything else you want to be seen – otherwise you don't exist! What your father saw with his hands was something you ended up hating. And your mother just let it happen, even though you were going to pieces right in front of her. Don't you see? Your parents made you invisible to yourself!' The blood was roaring in my head, and again I saw Agatha on the edge of the chair in her white house, a look on her face that no one should ever have to wear.

Her voice was fragile, and it sounded as though she was holding her breath as she asked, 'But what does that mean?'

Such a simple question. As I answered I was

painfully aware that I had precisely seventy-one sessions left before retirement, and that only six of them were with Agatha. Suddenly the number, which had always been too high, felt frighteningly low.

'It means you've got to learn to see yourself, Agatha.'

Figure/background

The funeral took place one Sunday morning. Madame Surrugue had sent an official invitation in the post, and I could find no solid reason not to go.

So there I stood amid the sunshine, clammy-handed in a black funeral suit that smelled of mothballs. People filed past me into the same church where my parents had been married and buried. Most were older mourners, wearing dark clothes and reverential faces, and many of them greeted me, although we only knew each other in passing.

I'd had the same experience at my parents' ceremony; I remembered all the sympathetic handshakes, the glances demanding something from me that I couldn't force to the surface. *Do you know death?*

Then Madame Surrugue arrived, pausing just in front of me. I stretched out my hand.

'My condolences.'

She took it and nodded. She was even thinner than last time I saw her, but her eyes were calm when they met mine.

'Thank you,' she said.

Her steps crunched over the gravel path that led the final stretch up to the church, and for a short moment I froze the image: a woman in black with a white church ahead of her. As she stepped through the double doors, black dissolved into black.

I followed my secretary into the church and sat down on a pew, the wood worn smooth. The interior was cool, and the distinctive scent of stone, wood and candles dry after the muggy warmth outside. Gradually other scents arrived: women's perfume, men's pomade and the nauseating sweetness of the lilies.

Would Madame Surrugue now return to the clinic and help with the last formalities? I hadn't dared discuss it with her during my visit, but there was only a week and a half to go before my retirement, and everything had to be arranged beforehand. The remaining patients had to be wrapped up or referred for treatment elsewhere, the files had to be organised so they could be passed on or archived, and the contract with the clinic's new owners wasn't yet finalised. Without her it would be an insurmountable task.

I tried again to focus on the ceremony. At the front of the church was the velvet-lined coffin. I wondered how he looked inside it, and whether he'd gone willingly in the end. Something told me he had.

I remained seated during the service, the priest's sermon and the four hymns, although a treacherous ache in my throat made it impossible to join in the singing, and the stench of the flowers grew heavier and heavier. It settled like a pain behind my eyes and bored beneath my skin, and as eight men in freshly pressed suits carried Thomas out something inside me broke.

A sob rose up in my throat, and I felt my face crumple. Instinctively I hid it in my hands, but my tears intensified, and I had to bite down hard on my thumb to muffle the plaintive sound forcing its way out.

I jumped as I felt an arm placed around my back.

My first impulse was to shake it off, but I didn't move.
Instead, to my own surprise, I remained sitting on the
hard pew with a stranger's arm around me, crying.

Peace

The day after the funeral I went down to Le Gourmand after work to buy ingredients for a cake.

Only once I was inside the shop and had found a basket did I realise I had no idea where to begin. Luckily a young woman with a blue-spotted scarf around her hair was standing behind the counter, filling a jar with boiled sweets, so I went up to her and cleared my throat.

'Please excuse the interruption, but might you be able to tell me how to bake a cake?'

The woman laughed out loud, revealing two

perfect dimples. 'Certainly I can. What kind of cake did you have in mind?'

'That's a good question,' I said. 'Something with apples?'

'An apple cake, we can manage that. Follow me!'

She led me among the shelves, finding flour, sugar and a pat of butter, offering me a stick of cinnamon to sniff and putting large brown eggs in my basket.

'The apples are over here,' she said, pointing out a few large baskets containing various fruits and vegetables. 'Do you have cardamom already?'

'I only have a little bread and an old cheese, I'm afraid.'

The woman laughed again. 'Then I think it's about time we expanded your range a little.'

She helped me with the rest of the ingredients while she explained that her father delivered fresh eggs to the shop every morning, and that the cake I was going to bake was based on a recipe of her deceased grandmother's, who had been known far and wide for her culinary skill.

'Who are you baking it for?'

'It's a kind of peace offering,' I explained, and she

nodded as though it were the most natural thing in the world.

Once all the items had been packed into brown paper bags, I thanked her repeatedly.

'It was my pleasure,' she smiled. 'Do you have any paper?'

Taking my pencil and the notepad I always kept in my bag, she began to write.

'Then you just need to let it cool down properly before serving. Then it'll be ready to make peace.'

There was flour everywhere. I didn't have a whisk, so it was a near-impossible task to get all the lumps out, even though I mixed as hard as I could. But once I was finished and the cake sat round and fragrant in my mother's old tin, the half-moon-shaped wedges of apple arranged in a spiral, I could barely contain my delight.

My heart thudded in my chest as I rang the bell. The door opened, and if he was surprised to see me he hid it well.

'Good afternoon,' I said, exaggerating the movements of my mouth, 'I've baked a cake.' I nodded at the dish and passed it towards him.

Finally I got a good look at my neighbour. He

was somewhere in his sixties, I'd guess, and rather more rotund than myself. He wore a dressing gown faded from washing, with grey, unruly hair and inch-thick spectacles on a cord around his neck. Perhaps I had disturbed him while reading the paper.

As he merely stood there blinking in confusion, I shouted, 'Cake!' with the same over-articulated enunciation as before.

Hesitantly he took the warm package, lifting it to his face as though to inhale the scent. An expression of surprise crossed his tired face. Then he slowly raised his hand to his heart, forming a clear *thank you* with his lips. All at once I thought he looked a dreadfully sorry sight with his protruding belly and the small tufts of hair bristling from his ears.

You exist, I wanted to say. *I listen when you play, just there, on the other side of the wall.*

Instead I nodded and raised an awkward hand in farewell: 'Don't mention it. See you again soon!'

Once I'd reached my own house, I turned. I was glad I did so. In the open doorway my neighbour was still standing with the cake pressed against his chest, his hand lifted in a wave.

Apple Cake

Melt most of the butter in a pan, making sure it doesn't burn.

Stir well with two heaped cups of sugar until pale, mixing in the four eggs as you go. Take four cups of flour, a pinch of salt and a teaspoon of baking soda and mix in a bowl. Add a little cardamom and snap the sticks of cinnamon and vanilla. Just scrape in as much of the contents as preferred. If desired, you can add a little milk as well.

Stir well, and voila – there's your dough. Grease a pan and pour in the dough, then press the peeled and chopped wedges of apple firmly into the dough. Drizzle with a pinch of sugar to taste.

The cake should be baked at 180 degrees for at least forty-five minutes. Let it cool for at least half an hour before serving.

Bon appetit!

Home

One morning I was lying underneath my warm eider-down, gazing up at the fine network of cracks in the ceiling as I played through the coming day. I was going to see five patients, and it occurred to me that at that precise moment I had no idea how many in total were still left to go.

In the kitchen I heated water in the kettle. Fetched the bag of black tea from the drawer, inhaled its scent and poured the dried leaves into a strainer. My neighbour was awake; he too was boiling water, for shortly afterwards I heard the characteristic howl of his kettle through the wall. Then I threw out the tea leaves, poured milk into the cup and ate a hasty breakfast at the kitchen table. Meanwhile I wondered how a deaf man had come to play the piano. Perhaps at some point he'd been able to hear; I'd have to ask him one day, if I dared.

'Good morning, Monsieur.'

I was so glad to see her that for the first time in my life I seized my secretary's shoulders in something rather like an embrace.

'How wonderful you're back,' I exclaimed, letting her go. 'You are back, aren't you?'

Madame Surrugue gave a bashful smile, looking every inch like a young girl being given her first compliment.

'D'you know, I think I am,' she replied. 'I've nothing more to do at home, so it was time.'

And then she took my stick – it was now too warm for a coat, even for me – and I placed my hat on the shelf.

'I have taken the liberty of adding a new patient to the schedule,' she said off-handedly, as she walked back to her chair.

'A new patient?' I cried after her. 'Oh, but you can't!'

'Nonsense,' she said, turning towards me. 'Surely you're not still intending to retire?'

She was looking at me so sharply that I hesitated. I had never found a good answer to the question of how I'd use the time once I stopped working. The countdown had been an end in itself, and beyond it? Nothing but empty mirrors.

Still, merely on principle I refused to acknowledge she was right so quickly. I sent her what I hoped was a censorious glance and said: 'You must consult me before you take these decisions, Madame Surrugue, you know that perfectly well. This simply will not do.'

She didn't look remotely guilty.

'I will consider the matter and get back to you this afternoon,' I said, and it's to my secretary's credit that I could barely see the tiny twitch around her mouth as she nodded and sat back on her throne.

Minimalistic order was restored on the great desk, and Madame Surrugue began to type at fearsome speed, her eyes fixed on the papers in front of her.

Agatha XII

She was walking ahead of me, perhaps fifteen yards distant. She wore black from head to toe, although it was a shimmeringly hot and shadeless day; only a narrow yellow ribbon in her hair stood out. I thought she was bewitching, but by now that should be obvious.

She walked swiftly and purposefully, and my weary old man's legs struggled to keep up, but suddenly she halted and whipped round. I stopped short. The sun burned against the sweat-drenched back of my shirt, and I thought: So, you've been caught. It's over now. Everybody knows you shouldn't mix therapy and real life; just look what it did to Jung.

She had paused right outside the café on the Boulevard des Reines, and now she stretched out a hand as though to push the glass door open, shading her eyes from the sun with the other. Her voice reached me with absolute clarity, although there were people between us on the pavement; although the gurgling waterfall in the garden where I'd hidden from her last time had been switched on. As though my ears were tuned to precisely her frequency.

'Well, Doctor,' she gestured towards the café with a little toss of her head. 'Are you coming, or what?'